The Giant Seeds

Story by Heather Hammonds

Illustrations by Richard Hoit

Mrs Miller said to her class,
"I would like you to bring
flower seeds to school tomorrow.
We will plant them, and water them,
and watch them grow."

"This could be fun,"
Becky whispered to Georgia.

But Georgia was wondering
what seeds she could bring.
Her family lived in an apartment,
and they didn't have a garden.

2

That evening,
Georgia asked her mother
if she had any plant seeds.

"You can have some of these,"
said Mum.
"I've been leaving them
on the windowsill to dry.
Here you are."

"They are **giant** seeds!"
said Georgia. "Thanks, Mum!"

The next day, the children
brought some seeds to school.
Georgia's were by far the biggest.
Everyone stared at them.

"What sort of seeds are **those**?"
Becky asked.

"They are giant seeds," answered Georgia.
"I'm going to have the biggest plants
in the class!"

But Mrs Miller said,
"Those are pumpkin seeds, Georgia."

Georgia suddenly remembered
that she hadn't told her mother
she needed **flower** seeds.

All the children looked at Georgia,
and she felt embarrassed.

Mrs Miller said kindly,
"You can plant your seeds, Georgia.
It doesn't really matter."

She handed out some plastic pots
and some soil.
She showed the children
how to plant their seeds
and how to water them.

At the end of the week,
Georgia saw two tiny pumpkin plants
peeping out of her pot.

"Look!" she cried.
"My plants have come up first!"

Georgia's plants grew very fast!
Soon they were too big for their pot.

Tiny plants began to come up
in the other pots.

But Georgia's plants kept on growing, too.
They grew longer and longer.
They grew all around the other pots
and down towards the floor!

"Oh, Georgia!" said Becky.
"Your pumpkin plants are climbing
into my pot!
They are going everywhere!"

Georgia wished she had flower plants
like everyone else.

11

One morning, Mrs Miller said,
"Our plants are big enough
to go in the school garden.
If we put them in now,
they will have flowers in time
for Parents' Day."

That afternoon,
the caretaker helped the children
to put their plants into the garden.
But when he saw Georgia's plants,
he said,
"These don't really belong here.
They're too big!
We'll have to put them
at the back of the garden
where they will have enough room."

Georgia felt disappointed
when she saw her plants in the garden.
They were flopping everywhere.

Every day, the children's plants
grew bigger and stronger.
Soon flowers began to appear.
Some were bright orange
and others were blue or purple.

"I wish some flowers would grow
on **my** plants," said Georgia,
looking at the leaves.

But Georgia's pumpkin plants
just kept on growing
at the back of the garden.

On the morning of Parents' Day,
the garden looked beautiful.
The children ran over
to have a closer look.
Then they all stopped and stared.
There, on Georgia's pumpkin plant,
were three huge golden flowers.
They were the biggest,
brightest flowers in the garden!

"Wow!" cried Georgia.
"My giant seeds
have grown **giant** flowers!"

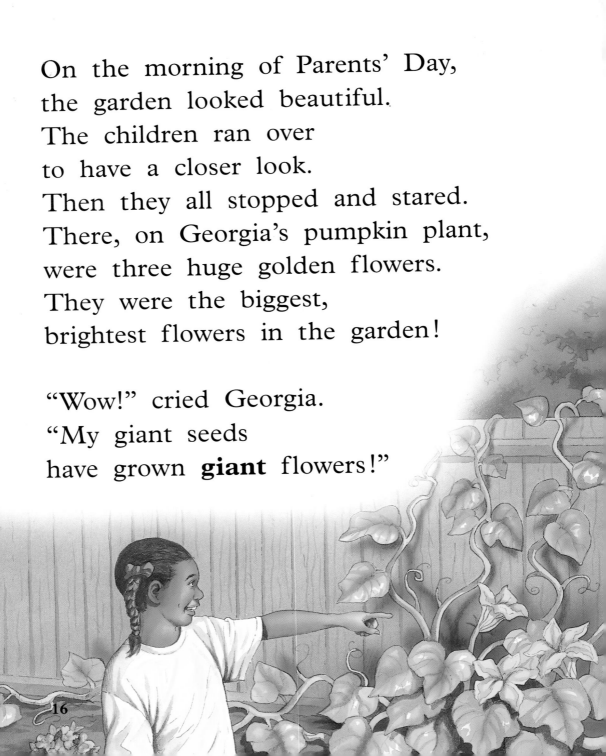